TO DANCE WITH A DEVIL

Julie Modla

Cover design and typesetting by Amanda Cummings.

Published by Amazon UK

www.juliemodla.com
Cheshire, United Kingdom

ISBN: 9798666044087

Acknowledgements

Shaping and crafting stories are one of the most intimate ways one can connect with another.

Books are wonderful ways of embarking on a new adventure and becoming lost in time.

As the words interlace and as each page is turned the fool embarks on his new journey.

I would like to thank Audrey Angus my true friend for encouraging me to live my dream of putting pen to paper.

Michael Koropisz, my inspiration for Edmund. A fine artist and portrait painter, pianist and historian, my guide on 19th century Britain.

To Jez and Nadia for patience as I embark on another writing journey.

To Ray Jenkinson my teacher. Thank you for all your inspiration. Without your teachings I'm not sure I would have written these books of truth.

Chapter One

Edmund Anthony Hall, an art dealer, a restorer of paintings and a fine artist within his own right, had taken lease of premises close to his home in the busy city of Manchester.

The address, one of Lever Street, an establishment reachable by taking the train into London Road Station city centre and walking down station approach a ten-minute stroll if that. It stood amongst a small row of tall buildings at the top and to the left of the street.

All gated, with worn steps that led down

to a basement, according to local history books, once, had homed tenants with families within these cellars, their abode during the 19th century. They lived in poverty, the floors above, occupied by tailors and seamstresses turning out garments for the rag trade, the tailors created fine suits for distinguished gents.

The ground floor had now been leased to Edmund, he, so excited to create his dream; a gallery, his very own place to display his and others works of art, a room at the back for restoration of these wonders.

Work had to be done in this back room as the floor had rotted and needed repair. Plaster peeled from the walls but this did not phase him and he happily engaged local builders to carry out these restorations as this was not his forte at all.

Artists would come and go to purchase canvases, paints, varnishes and display their creations alongside his own, a proper mini art gallery within the city centre.

A radio played dance music in the background as he busied himself within his studio, a regular start to a young fool's day. What a purchase! Pride and pleasure as he placed his collections on easels and freshly painted walls. Excited, as he had planned a promotion, local artists were involved and the local press would be there. The general public and many important guests would be at the launch as Edmund was a member of an affluent lodge called 'The Club' within the city centre.

A meeting took place once a month, twenty-six would gather, all professionals within their own right. Writers, doctors, solicitors, judges amongst others. He a fine member of this lodge.

Eager to impress his counterparts and

feeling as proud as punch, and now regarded highly within his affluent circle of friends.

The trouble was, on the other hand, the fool had borrowed an excessive amount of money from a dealer, a money lender; a man recommended by one of his friends at 'The Club'.

Lost in the excitement of launching and driving his new business off the ground, he had foolishly not read the small print as he signed on the dotted line. A regret, as it had unfortunately stated that interest on the loan could fluctuate at the convenience of the lender.

As he tried to make payments every month on his loan, the balance just would not go down. Dismayed, he found it was increasing month by month.

The gallery had drawn a fair amount of interest from the general public. After the opening, folk would browse through the window or enter the shop with awe to take a look. Most though, were not so quick enough to dig deep into their pockets in exchange for a picture.

As if things couldn't get much worse, he found he was struggling to pay back his lenders. The money dealer had started to pursue him. A business, hit and miss with sales and interest rates so high, a secret struggle, a pressure, constant, with very little money to do so.

A feeling of sickness rose in his gut, as persistent, pestering thoughts troubled his peace of mind. Living beyond his means with borderline poverty, his loyal friend, his dog, looked sadly up at him and gave a grave sigh. He had no idea what to do? His lease signed with no way out, a secret struggle, a secret he hoped would not be made public, hoping only to be shared with himself and his money dealer.

A scandal he didn't want! Desperate, his head in hands, a fist slammed down on an old wooden counter he gaped to the drawer of his empty open till.

Wringing his hands in despair, the postman broke his thoughts as another unwelcome envelope landed on his mat. Reaching down into the recess of the heavy drawer within his counter, immediate comfort was felt as his hand reached, searched and gripped the smooth sensual neck of his half empty whisky bottle.

Top twisted off, as the pleasurable sound of glug, glug, glug, glug, the amber nectar poured into the heavy crystal glass. The glass, a persona he showed to the outside world.

The strong smell of bourbon reached his nostrils and he took a gulp of the spirit, a sharp taste burnt and stung his tongue as the elixir ran down his throat and the immediate warmth consumed him.

His dog looked at him rather sadly and deep inner voices called and shouted to him. He took no heed, yes, without a doubt the whisky would take hold of him but just for now he would deal with that, as this was the only thing taking the edge off his worries. So, he sank another drink and stooped to pick up the other letter to add to his pile of already unopened ones with a sigh.

Although, this was different somehow, the feel of the paper, thick, smooth, a letter sent to impress. A design embellished within the heavy paper; handwriting formal, interesting, as it had been sealed with a red wax stamp. A stamp with a symbol on it.

He fingered the seal with interest, feeling the stamp under his thumb. Initials or a symbol, he was quite sure he had seen this somewhere before.

This was no ordinary letter and certainly not a demand for money, a piece of correspondence that was to be opened immediately. Written in a cursive style, legible, spider-like, intricate and refined.

Sliding his thumb under the seal, he read this:

Dear Edmund,

Firstly, allow me to introduce myself. I am Eleanor of Wheatfield House, in the County of Linkshire.

I have been recommended to contact you by a good friend of mine, whom, I can't disclose at present.

He tells me you are a fine art restorer who may have fallen on difficult times.

Forgive my presumptions. However, I require a professional to restore and value some unique art work. Theses pieces belong to my brother and I.

I would want you to stay here at Wheatfield house, until you have completed the task. You can have no doubt that you will be paid more than handsomely for your work.

Waiting in anticipation for your reply

Eleanor. Lady of Wheatfield.

Chapter Two

With an air of excitement and a new found energy, Edmund replied back to the Lady and without too much consideration accepted the offer. An answer to his prayers he thought.

Plans were put into place; his niece would man the gallery and care for his dog while Edmund booked his train ticket a day or so later and off he headed for Linkshire.

He would stay one night at an Inn close to the train station as he would arrive early evening on a Friday night and would be collected by car, the following morning by a driver from Wheatfield House.

The Inn a few hundred years old, typical of a British pub. White rendered walls, thatchers had done an amazing job restoring the roof, square framed sash windows lit up and welcomed him in.

A chilly night, and as he entered, the open fire brought comfort to him.

Immediately, the hum and chatter from the busy bar mixed with the smell of hops, drifted up his nostrils and he ordered a well-earned pint of beer, alongside the speciality of the day, meat, potato and vegetables encased in a crisp pastry wrap.

Locals had gathered to drink and be merry, and more than welcomed and included him in their cheer.

A belly full, and after a couple of more drinks the feeling of tipsiness and warmth overcame him. loose tongues, conversations and laughter commenced. The bartender asked Edmund what was the purpose of his visit. Edmund explained that he had work to do, the restoration of some art work and would be leaving the following day for Wheatfield House.

The bartender stopped talking and looked dubiously to a man standing next to him and conversation was cut dead in its tracks. The conversation went something like this:

'...I'd warn you to steer clear from that place if I were you sir. I'd get back on the next train to where you came from if you know what's best for you. You don't want to get involved in what goes on up there I can tell you.'

The other man backed him up, 'strange goings on up at Wheatfield, there's talk of an unusual bunch, some kind of secret society, regular visitors I'd say... talk has it there is a masquerade ball, mentions of rituals and all that occult...'

His conversation was cut short by the door of the Inn being flung open. The silhouette of a man in a dark suit and bowler hat. A chill followed him in from the cold evening air. A presence. Edmund sensed the atmosphere had changed and the merriment ceased as the man approached the bar. Sinister, his voice as warm as a tomb. Cold, hostile eyes, a lords nose, he gave a sneer as the locals backed away.

As they dispersed the man took his seat, ordered his Chablis and threw his coins on the bar.

Not someone he fancied socialising with he thought, so he ordered a night cap of port to take up to his room and left the man, who had caused the disturbance and lack of merriment to retire for the night.

He pondered as to why those folks had stopped talking when the man had made his presence known.

Superstition he concluded, and made his way to his bedroom. A room quaint, window sills that barely came up to his knees. There was no need to close the drapes as he wasn't overlooked.

Choppy was the night, the wind whipped up autumn leaves in a frenzy, he changed into his nightwear, climbed into the cold fresh cotton white sheets, brought his knees up to his chest to keep warm and quickly fell into a deep sleep.

A slumber disturbed, something sobered and woke him like a slap. On checking his time piece, he was irritated to find it was only half past three. Wondering as to what had woken him so suddenly he climbed out of bed, crossed the room to the low sill of his bedroom window and on rubbing his eyes, glanced out into the inky night sky, astounded to see what looked like a convoy of cars heading north, away from the road that he was to travel to by car the following morning.

An unusual sight to see at this ungodly hour, headlights lighting up the gravel below, past the Inn. No ordinary cars were these, but prestige vehicles, ranging from Rolls Royce, Bentleys, Aston Martins amongst many.

Clambering back into his now warm bed he entered into a fairly interrupted sleep, until tired he woke. He dressed, gathered his belongings including the equipment he had brought for the restoration, and made his way back into the bar area. He was to wait there for his lift to start his new project, one of which would add massive status to his business within the art world.

Chapter Three

A frosty silent journey commenced as the driver had no need for small talk. He had his instructions to carry out, and that's just exactly what he would do.

Neither curious, nor interested as to why this visitor had been engaged. Non of his business, he did his job and asked no questions. The visitor very quickly sensed this, so he settled into the luxury of the soft leather seat. Nothing like the scent of a new car, especially one as plush as this. He sat back and took in the Linkshire scenery.

The roads wound through greenery,

countryside and trees. Such a refreshing change from the grim industrial greyness of Manchester, where fogs that resembled pea soups were the norm. He noticed there were no other houses to be seen, fairly isolated, unlike the Inn he had stayed at, that was, until they turned a bend in the road and there, magnificent, it dominated the vista. A house so grand, certainly that of a stately home. Built in a silvery grey Pentewan stone. An 18th century mansion.

Formal gardens surrounded the place, some areas neat and manicured. Parts towards the right of the perimeter, woody and overgrown. The owners obviously liked sculptures and many were placed in areas of their choice. Not a fan, they reminded him of something you would find looking over sleeping angels in a cemetery. Quite a contrast from the autumn leaves of the rhododendrons, azaleas, and mature trees where the grounds seemed to sweep down to what looked like a lake of some sort. This was the residence of some aristocrat for sure.

They approached and drove down the gravelly drive, the sound of the stones crunched under the tyres and he was aware that at least four dogs and a groundsman were in the vicinity. The dogs, descendants of the wolf;dogs, known to put their lives in danger for the sake of their owner. He felt reassured, as the man called them to heel, none on leads but obedient and loyal.

Large heavy panelled oak doors were opened. He was formally greeted at the door by the front of house, smartly dressed, a suit with tails, his luggage was swiftly taken and he was led through long corridors lined by magnificent artworks, many of those being portraits, he assumed they were the ancestors and family members.

Edmund ignored the indifference to his arrival and eager to explore these wonders, he settled into his room. Large, more of a suite, with a wooden four poster bed, it was decorated in lemon and white hues but he was more interested in the model, the actress portrayed in various poses hung in frames around the room. Beautiful, he noticed a sadness within her eyes, every picture spoke of an unhappiness. He wondered as to her story.

He sat in the recess of the large bay window and admired the view. He was feeling quite privileged to have been employed there at such a grand place. His luck had turned he thought.

A note on the mahogany table requested that he join Eleanor and Victor the Baron for dinner at seven. He was given permission to explore the first and second floor but not to enter the grounds without an escort as the dogs were loose. Tomorrow he was to become acquainted with the paintings.

Chapter Four

Edmund made his way down the grand oak staircase which wound itself down into the hall. He was directed into the rather cosy dining room which boasted a large oval mahogany table, it was French polished to resemble that of a mirror.

Victor eased around the room with an air of confidence and then seated himself at one end of the oval. He noted a sense of arrogance around the Baron. His eyes shining with hostility, as passionless as that of an executioner he thought. Handsome enough, slicked back hair with a firm jaw. A place set out for Edmund and one place set out for another.

They must be expecting someone to join us he thought. Just to break his thinking the front of house in his black and white tails opened the door and escorted, in, no other than the man with the bowler hat he had seen previously at the Inn. The very same man who had, had, the uncomfortable presence to clear the villagers from the bar with nothing else but his aura.

Edmund was already seated, politely he rose from his seat to greet and shake the man's hand. The man just nodded and a strange evening began. Rebuffed Edmund sat back down. What an odd atmosphere he thought.

The clock ticked loudly in contrast as the Baron and the man nodded to each other and both chose not to speak.

They proceeded to be taking a perverse pleasure in studying and weighing him up. He had never come across such weird behaviour, a strange exchange from the two. Uncomfortable to say the least.

Eleanor, his sister, slim with a queenly air; eyebrows plucked pencil thin, the fashion of the time. Ginger auburn hair, jade dewy eyes and a cheerful character seemed unaffected by the behaviour of the other two. She broke the ice and proceeded to chatter, unaffected by the silence in the room.

To Edmunds relief she asked questions and shared the reasons that she had asked him to come and why he had been brought here and what she would have him do.

All the while, the other two occasionally made eye contact but ate the fine meal in silence.

A feast of venison accompanied by ruby red wine, decanted and poured into heavy crystal glasses.

The sister instructed the art restorer to stay

at the house until his work was done. There were twelve paintings. He was only allowed to see them one at a time.

Edmund responded that he looked forward to starting his task.

She carried on in stating that there was a reason for this but it would only unravel and become apparent as the work progressed. A room would be allocated to him and he could work at his leisure, however, as long as the work was complete by the end of the month.

Eager to leave this strange bunch, Edmund agreed to her requirements; under normal circumstances he may have refused this job, due to the atmosphere of the place. Although, these were not normal circumstances and he needed the handsome wage that she was offering, to pay the money lender, so agree he did.

As an observer, Edmund looked upon the Barons friendship with the man as odd. He noticed they had their differences but despite that, there seemed a strong link holding them together he thought.

Edmunds off handed welcome was bizarre in itself, as the art connoisseur was amicable, and had arrived with a drive and an enthusiasm to restore their artworks. No need for the frosty reception he thought.

As the Baron inhaled his after dinner cigar and took a large sip of his cognac, Edmund was aware of the hosts cynical smile to his other male guest. Although, the smile did not reflect in his jet black eyes.

His persona was powerful and virile, his handsome face took on an excited look as his other guest crushed an unsuspecting moth with his thumb.

The four sat and stared at each other as

Eleanor busied herself wiping up the left overs of the moths wings and crushed body from the table. Talking about not very much indeed, trying to break the atmosphere within the room. The Baron in the mean time flicked his fat cigar ash onto the floor in total disregard then placed it on the silver standard ashtray. He kicked his chair back and rang the bell to summon the butler and with an airy gesture ordered more of his finest cognac.

Edmund glanced from the sallow face of the guest to the Baron who's eyes didn't smile and took this as his queue to leave, he bid the three goodnight while thinking it odd that the guest hadn't even been introduced to him, nor he to him, he figured that it was none of his business and he would refer to him as the man in the bowler hat in the hope that he wouldn't have to go through the unsociable intercourse with this man again. He left the room to retire for the night to his suite.

As if the evening hadn't been strange enough, as he left, he heard raised male voices along with Eleanor laughing and talking amongst themselves. He couldn't quite hear the conversation as the door to the dining room was heavy and thick. There was no doubt his ears were not playing tricks on him.

He made his way up to his room. He looked out into the blackness of the night and was aware of the prowling of the hounds. He could sleep comfortably with a knowing, they could all sleep safely within their beds, as no one would try and get past that pack of canines.

Chapter Five

Edmund was up bright and early and after taking breakfast in his room, headed eagerly to the studio that had been allocated to him on the same landing.

He was a true professional with great confidence that he would be able to do the best job possible and couldn't wait to see these works of art.

The studio was ample for his requirements and well stocked, with all he had asked for. There was enough natural light and there were black heavy drapes, should he need to work in the dark.

A large easel boasted itself, in the centre of the fairly empty room. An ornate door led off to another, but on trying the handle he found it was locked.

The picture stood covered with a large black velvet cloth that hid the masterpiece. He unveiled it to discover that the painting, ornately framed was dark, yellow, with varnish that was cracked.

The reason this happened to these pieces was usually down to the climate in which they were stored, and the varnish Dammar, a varnish that was still used then even by Edmund. It was known to crack and darken paintings usually after around thirty years or so. So, his evaluation was, that this piece had been painted around 1890. This, he concluded meant, that the aristocracy or someone quite wealthy had commissioned this oil painting. As around the 1890's photography had become very fashionable, and was far more cheaper than commissioning an artist to paint for them.

Edmund poured out and prepared his turpentine substance in which to remove the old Dammar. This would brighten and restore the art work first. Edmund would then re-varnish and bring this painting back to life.

Tirelessly and meticulously he began the intricate process, and as morning turned into afternoon the eeriness and beauty of the picture revealed itself to him.

What a unusual scene confronted him. A room dark and gloomy, candelabras on the walls, dimly warmed the space. A large door, ornately carved with symbols he could barely make out. The door was ajar and he could just make out the large stone steps leading up to somewhere else.

A heavy table, covered with a navy-blue cloth; there sat a man at the very table, his back facing the viewer. He had dark hair and wore a black jacket. The strange thing was he appeared to be gazing into a black mirror and even more unnerving was the face who stared back at him, was a hazy reflection of a female.

Mesmerised he stared at her, her features faint due to the ribbons of wavy wisps, and the clouds that surrounded her. He jolted back into the room as he was sure she turned and smiled at him.

Those chemicals he had been using he was sure, had gone to his head and he needed to take some fresh air. He had been working non stop and needed to stretch his legs.

He was satisfied with what he had achieved for the day and closed his studio.

He made his way downstairs and opened the large front door. He would go for a stroll around the grounds. He headed off towards the woodland area that was at the right of the large lawn, a nice refreshing change to the city life.

His shoes snapped on the twigs and dirt underfoot, he breathed in the earthy smells and listened as the birds chirped and communicated together. Music to his ears. He could live this life he thought. The trees weren't too dense. It was late afternoon, he wouldn't venture too far as it would be going dark soon. He was enjoying the change of scenery. Until he heard a noise, and he realised he wasn't alone.

He felt it more than he heard it. Edmund feared for his safety as a strange feeling came over him and his skin went cold as the presence made itself known.

A twig snapped and he saw menacing amber eyes followed by a deep low growl. He wanted to run but at the same time he was glued to the spot. Everywhere he looked, he was trapped, he was too far away from the house. A feeling of sheer panic gripped his chest and he struggled to breathe.

There was nowhere to run, he was trapped and rooted to the ground. Within split seconds Edmund looked to see if the trees could offer any safety. They were old and wide with nowhere to even climb, as the dog barred its teeth, snarled and lowered itself in order to pounce.

He couldn't take his eyes off this creature. This snarling animal was primal, savage and powerful.

Last night, he had felt protected by, this illusion of safety; today was now his enemy.

Edmund knew that if he turned and ran the beast would be on him faster than a whippet, he also knew he was certainly no match for this killer.

Sweating with fright, his breathing came faster now with the fear of being ravaged and torn apart, a deep terror for his fate as another twig snapped. Turning quickly without taking his eyes off this dog the welcome site of the grounds man appeared, he moved slowly and firmly towards the dog and closed wooden dog containers to the anger of the beast who wriggled, struggled and barked at its containment.

'Next time you might not be so lucky, I might not always be on duty, these dogs are driven by instinct. They are trained to kill. Don't you ever think these dogs aren't within the grounds. They will sniff out all that is not familiar to them. I would advise you to go back into the house and if you want a tour of the grounds I can show you round sir.'

Edmund couldn't thank the groundsman enough. He bid the man good day and turned, shaking and relieved left the man to calm and pacify the beast.

Chapter Six

Glad to be within the comfort of his chamber and relieved that he wasn't meeting his maker just yet, he washed his hands and face in cold water to cool him down after his fright.

On the table close to the window he noticed an envelope addressed to him. Lying next to it a brown card board box. He slid his thumb under the seal and found it to contain an invitation to a masked ball this evening within the grand hall. A black tie affair, masks to be provided.

Edmund opened the box and just as

he expected it contained a face covering. His, a pigs head. Unusual, an animal theme he thought to himself. Amused he made his way to the chair near the window to read the daily tabloid.

Gazing up from his newspaper, he had to look twice, as a convoy of prestige cars, the ones he had seen once before while staying at the Inn, were slowly making their way up the long drive to the house.

That explains it, Victor and Eleanor must have these parties on a regular basis, as it was only a week or so, he thought when he last saw them. He was going to enjoy this, as his stay here had been pretty dull up to know.

Chapter Seven

A couple of hours later Edmund made his way down to the ball, still amused to be wearing the mask of a pig. A little self conscious but intrigued as to what the other guests would be.

Everyone seemed to be wearing various animal adornments even the quartet, playing the dance music of the times, in the corner of the large room. Edmund loved to hear music and was looking forward to joining in.

The waiter handed him a silver tray with beautiful crystal flutes of fine champagne and he looked around the room. Twelve guests laughed and talked to each other. Six of which where females. His eyes studied the masks as he tried to figure out which one was Eleanor. Until, a red haired woman wearing the mask of a lioness took his hand and proceeded to introduce him to everyone.

Edmunds eyes flickered and grazed the guests within the room.

The woman of a mature age, expensively dressed in a long turquoise velvet gown, a ring, Cartier, one of the most prestigious jewellers of the Art Deco era, the jewel of considerable value adorned her fourth finger. Her mask, a swan.

She regarded him for a moment as a podgy man with wiry white hair lit her cigarette. She looked at him at first with interest and then turned coldly away, as the little man almost fell over himself to please her. Her disregard obvious to all but the man in the cows mask.

Next, a small podgy lady in an ill fitting lace dress observed him. She had arrived as a dog.

The Hen, he observed was flirting obsessively with the Raven, not a match, he concluded amused.

To save the awkwardness of protecting her art restorer from this beastly bunch the Barons sister grabbed his arm and guided him over to a panther.

Eleanor introduced him to a glamorous woman with beautiful dark hair her, skin bronzed, from some far exotic place. 'Antonia, meet my dear friend Edmund, he is an art expert, the best within his field.'

Her figure tall slender and graceful. Lifted her hand for him to place a kiss on. Her skin was beautiful and perfumed.

An exotic accent he suspected to be Spanish.

His eyes were fixed on her, and he was

curious and excited to know if under her mask, her beauty paired with her voice. Dark and sensual, someone passed him a drink as he fixed on this femme fatale and sipped, as did she.

She seemed to take a powerful pleasure in flirting with him. Edmund was in no position to resist, her power over him was magnetic. He had no ability to object, as he found her to be highly desirable. She shared her life story how she became one of the most desired actresses in Brazil.

Her story was fascinating. How this starlet was plucked from obscurity, to become one of the most famous faces in South America.

Hank Marx from a national film company was on vacation in Rio when he came across her in a café. He helped her launch her career. Staring in the black and white moving pictures, alongside side the famous faces of Hal Pearson,

Orson Hewitt and Lawrence Portman.

Edmund was impressed to learn that Antonia Silva had starred in *The Steel Point* (1920) and *Letters from Cane* (1922). Edmund was not a fan of the big screen. Although he had read about these films in his tabloid. He preferred the theatre and the Free Trade Hall was one of the favourite places he liked to go to at weekends. So when she removed the mask she wore, it didn't make any difference as to recognition.

Her eyes, dark and sensual connected with his, as someone passed him a drink. He sipped, while fixated upon her, she had a way of giving him her full attention. They moved out of the ball through the French doors onto the steps of the balcony.

It had become a little stuffy in the room and they welcomed the brisk autumn air as Edmund removed his mask. Both were not disappointed. Edmunds well defined cheekbones and blue eyes flickered with curiosity. Antonia gazed into the eyes of this handsome vigour of youth who radiated such energy.

Her long ruby red finger nails gently brushed against his wrist and her touch jolted him like a current of electricity. This amazon beauty with sable black hair and demure personality was enticing and alluring to him.

Even before the kiss he knew what she was doing. Seduction was what Antonia did best, she moved into Edmunds personal space, where she didn't just look at the man, she looked into the man. There was no resistance from Edmund when she brushed his lips with hers.

Then just as if nothing had happened between them she made the excuse that it was chilly and they should go back to the others.

Edmund was on fire as he followed her back into the room, his eyes eased the full length of her body. A sculptor could not have created such a flawless bronzed skin and shape.

This woman was wild with mystique. As she glanced back at him her eyes were smouldering. Full of passion, but he knew she was playing a game with him. She was the cat and he was the mouse.

Edmund helped himself to another drink and made conversation with the Raven who he found out was a dentist from London. He had his own practice and was a regular visitor here. His conversation was rather dull and all the while Edmunds thoughts were on the temptress.

Within a few minutes, his eyes started searching frantically around the room as he started to feel very unwell.

A hot pumping sensation moved through

his temples. A pulsing within his head. He couldn't understand how he could feel so tipsy on two glasses of champagne. He needed some fresh air really quickly.

As the hot blood within his body circulated around his face and his body, his eyes blurred as the guests seemed to be moving in towards him.

He started to make his way anxiously to the French doors as he started to feel very sick.

The last thing he remembered was his brain on fire and that's when he blacked out.

What seemed like hours later, with his head pounding he woke up naked in his bed. Stumbling he searched for his dressing gown, confused and feeling sick he reached for the first thing he could find and retched up last nights dinner onto the pigs head in his wastepaper bin.

Perplexed and wondering as to how he

had ended up blacked out with no clothes on in his bed. He tried to clarify his situation, he could hear noises on the landing outside, he unsteadily ventured out to see who was there and if anyone could help with what had happened.

Edmund was surprised to see the backs of hooded, robed figures making their way up the far end of the dimly lit landing, out through a doorway at the far end.

Curious and dubious, he was intrigued to see if these were the guests that had been at the party. As he approached the door he was aware that it had been left ajar. Purposely or not, he wasn't sure. There were heavy stone steps that led up to a room, with a banister that curved around the top and, he found he could sit on the stair, unobserved as he took in the scene within the room.

He heard before he saw, the sound of

chanting. Strange incantations were being muttered quietly within the space. There he witnessed a scene not unlike those within the artwork.

Faceless hooded frames. Mumbling unusual words, unnerving within the gloom, a circle containing two interlinked triangles painted white on a black floor, a man turned to face the room, a ram's head where his face should have been and he raised a chalice above his head and spoke to the circle.

'Brothers and sisters we gather on that special day of the calendar once more, and we come together in unity to celebrate the events that lay waiting for us. The predictions I have foreseen.

For within this space we honour the immaterial force and astral power of the great one...'

One of the hoods turned directly towards him and he was pretty sure he had been seen.

Turning and hurrying away quickly, he ran down the hallway, and panted breathlessly into his bedroom, he shut and locked the door. His back rested against the heavy wooden frame as he tried to recover his breath. Ear pressed against the door to see if he had been followed.

He was pretty sure he hadn't but Edmund was extremely disturbed by what he had witnessed; some sort of strange cult, his mind returned to that night at the Inn where he was sure the landlord and the regular customer, were trying to warn him off working at this house.

He recalled the man in the bowler hat who had cleared the pub that night the strange friend of the Baron. Could it possibly have been him wearing the Rams head.

Memories started to return to him, he started to have flash backs of two robed females undressing him, he wanted to stop them but he had no ability to, as his limbs felt too heavy and cement like.

The Spanish accent of the woman who had pretty much seduced him breathed and whispered gently in his ear while the other seemed nervous, she kept on checking the door.

Quietly, she asked him, 'are you awake? Edmund... wake up... please... wake up Edmund. You need to get away from this house very soon... please do as I tell you... it's not safe...'

He recalled them leaving him there, and again he blacked out again to only waken when the drug had worn off. It had to have been a sedative as he was used to drinking alcohol.

He couldn't guess why someone would have done that, for what reason? Was it to keep him out of the way while those guests performed their strange rituals?

He guessed this odd bunch were the reason why she had warned him to leave this place, she probably had a good point, and Edmund vowed that he would leave them to it, after all, he should be finished soon and he would just get on with it. The money was driving him to stay and finish what he had set out to do. Plus the status he would receive in the art world. Both were his driving force.

Tired and groggy but too scared to sleep, he sat on his bed upright and waited for dawn to come.

Chapter Eight

The following morning he headed on down to the breakfast room to find that the Baron and his guests had already left. Eleanor talked to him about anything and everything apart from the night before. Asking how he had been getting on with the painting.

The incident wasn't mentioned, not by her, nor by him, and he picked at his breakfast with no appetite, he answered that he had four left to restore which should take him another week or so and then he could return back to his gallery.

Hungry to get this work done, keen to

finish the restoration and return to some sanity. Also, eager for the handsome sum of money he had been promised to enable him to pay his money lender back in full.

Painting by painting he worked flat out, as day turned to night, the days went by and the interesting thing was that each one had the same thread, from the first to the twelfth. A man and a woman featured in every one of them and in each one they both had their faces hidden from the viewer.

A mystery. Why did the oil painter not want them to be seen. More interesting than that, who was or is this artist? How had Edmund not seen these works of art before. They were excellent pieces just mysterious and sinister.

The thread seemed to go something like this. From the first where the man gazed into a scrying mirror with a hazy female reflection.

The same couple appeared within different scenes, sometimes alone and sometimes with others, all with their faces hidden.

This time the man was sat looking at some manuscripts with strange lettering, a pen in hand. The girl casually resting her hand on the mans shoulder. A silver bracelet circled her wrist, set with an Egyptian eye.

Every painting, a tale unfolded. A wall down the centre of the image acted as a divider into two rooms. Interesting as the room on the left the female was crouched down to peer through a key hole in the door, on the other side the man carried a heavy metal key, the ornate Egyptian eye again set into the bow, just above the shoulder.

The pattern went on, fascinated Edmund poured more turpentine into the bowl and carried on. The eye was prevalent in the all the works he had uncovered. He placed the paintings next to each other in the order he had been given them.

The final one for the day was an intimate and disturbing one of the man in long dark grey robes, both his arms raised into the air, in his hand was a dagger pointing down at the woman's head as she knelt in front of him, naked, her head bowed down in submission.

The pommel above the blade carried the eye of the Egyptian. Her wrists were loosely bound by ropes in front of her. Both of them were encased within a circle surrounding two triangles interlinked. A room very similar to the one he had witnessed that evening, the one that he thought he had been drugged.

As the days passed by, Edmund became obsessed with the stories these paintings unveiled. He noticed the same thread, the same man and woman. There were also other people too, and as the pattern predicted none showed their faces.

There were books with writing, although this strange script was impossible to decipher. Edmund concluded it was either Greek or Hebrew. He, however, was not proficient in the translation of foreign languages.

He became obsessed and visited the library within the grand house and spent many hours within his studio alongside his restorations, flicking through large bound books that confounded him, with literature, intrigued by the ones, that spoke of strange occult practices.

The book that particularly excited him was *The Book of the Golden Order* – the prophesy. Published by Johnson & Richmond, London, 1868-1872 in three volumes as *Part 1* (1868) *Part 2* (1869) and *Part 3* (1872).

It was an account of teachings, rites and rituals and ceremonies of some dark forces. Occult meaning hidden, a belief in an unseen dimension. It talked of occult sciences using alchemy, astrology and spiritualism which was quite popular during these times. People would engage a medium and have parlour games at their homes. Many of these mediums were pure charlatans praying on grieving widows for money.

These volumes noted that the occultism, professed to essentially attempt to enlighten a disenchanted world. They openly distanced themselves from mainstream faiths.

It was an interesting read. Edmund was christened at birth and attended the local church and Sunday school as a boy and had his own religious beliefs, however, it didn't stop him being fascinated by what these books contained.

As he flicked the pages for more information he was astounded when he came across a collection of sketches. The illustrations he discovered were exact prints of those within the paintings.

There among the sketches the artists name was written. It was Albert Barolo Francis and the collection was no other than *The Power of the Hidden*. This was unbelievable! These art works were priceless. The artist didn't sign his work in the traditional sense but instead he had a symbol that he hid within the oil painting. It would be found in various places.

He jumped up from his chair and studied each piece, if these were the originals then the symbols would be there. Sure enough as Edmund pedantically searched and traced his experienced fingers over the new varnish. His eyes, watering as he concentrated. To his delight he discovered the first. It was there within the collar of the mans jacket.

It was a serpent that formed a circle, contained within the circle was an ankh and a star. Numbers revealed a date 1895.

Anticipation that the next portrait would be the last one judging by the sketches. He had already completed and restored eleven, and there were twelve according to this book.

He studied the twelfth sketch. The artist viewed the room that was next. A prediction of what was to be revealed. A room resembling a temple of sorts.

Thirteen stone thrones seated twelve robed figures, heads were lowered, covered by hoods, cloaks that revealed black ovals for faces. The same black symbolism painted upon the black slate floor. One throne empty. On the table left of a central robed figure, lay a dagger, and a chalice.

Chapter Nine

He was correct in his presumptions, as the final piece was brought to his studio the following day. The Barons sister seemed more nervous that morning and proceeded to potter around the morning room. Busying herself with dusting and rearranging the ornaments.

He mentioned that to her it was the last painting and he would be making his was back to Manchester within a day or so.

She insisted that he should take advantage of their hospitality and stay until after the weekend.

He agreed and decided, that, that evening

he would explore more of the house. There were pieces along the main corridor that totally fascinated him by some famous artists. There were ornaments and sculptures from foreign lands. Consumed with wonder at these collections he carried on down the long corridor.

Carved ornate doors, closed to him as he ventured on. Tapestries told tales of medieval wars, faded by the years and with contact with daylight. The texture of the wool used to create these stories felt soft to touch.

As his mind wondered about the creators, intricately sewing and chattering the hours away with each other, as they passed the time. He could imagine that there would have been several people working on them. He approached the end of the gallery and became aware of stone steps similar to that in the last painting.

As he climbed the steps they curved round, deep heavy steps. Opening out into a large throned room. Thirteen cold stone chairs he counted.

As his curiosity got the better of him he cautiously ventured forward.

Horrified he came across an alter of sorts. There were symbols, ropes, and a large dagger the very same as he had discovered in Franco's artwork.

Another smaller room led off from there, full of boxes ornaments and books. A storage room. There were fabrics and old moth eaten curtains, a musty old room. He carefully opened the boxes and took out the old volumes protected from many years of dust. He sat on a small foot stool to flick through the pages. There were some old picture books and children's novels.

There was a collection of five small leather

books bound together and tied in a bow by string. He opened it carefully to find these were diaries written by the Barons sister as a young girl. He slipped them into his inside pocket they looked an interesting read. They might throw some light on these strange people.

Just as he lifted the lid on a small wooden box the sound of male voices startled him, the door was ajar and he could make out the Baron talking to the butler.

'What did you say to the girl?'

'Exactly what I was instructed to say sir, that she was to travel here and take up a job as a maid to your sister. I gave her parents the money as instructed and she is settled at the moment.'

'Are my guests ready?'

Edmund was just able to glimpse the scene that was about to take place.

'Yes everything is in order, and the fowl

were delivered first thing this morning.'

'Splendid, let the festivities begin.'

'I will show them in sir, will there be anything else?'

'No.'

The Barons attire was that of the night Edmund had been drugged. A long robe, he started arranging some tools on the alter and pulled the hood over his head. He heard the chants before he saw them, the figures entered the room one by one, disguised by the cloaks. They circled around the Baron who drank from a large cup and then passed it around the group in an anti clockwise direction.

The chants were not in a language that Edmund understood. Careful not to be seen, as he couldn't very well make his presence known, not now he had witnessed this strange intimate affair between this bunch.

Edmund gasped with horror as one of

the men in the hooded robes gestured that the Baron opened the door to the temple. A young girl no more than eighteen years old was shoved and pushed in by the butler.

Her hands were bound by ropes, she wore a white cotton dress resembling a shroud and he motioned for her to be seated on a heavy stone slab.

Her legs were clenched tight together and she was shaking uncontrollably, her mouth gagged and her frightened eyes searched the room for help. The man spoke.

'Sacrifices are much more pleasant in the autumn don't you think?'

She starred at her feet her breath becoming more laboured with panic.

His mouth curled up into a smile, and he spoke with a cold, sadistic glint in his eyes.

'My dear child, you tremble.' He caressed her long dark hair, as his fingers traced along her throat, neck and the top of her milky white breasts.

'You find the evening chilly?' She recoiled from his touch. 'Perhaps we can wrap a shawl around those exquisite porcelain shoulders of yours.'

Two hooded men stepped forward and untied her wrists they lifted her up and laid her down on the large stone slab. They used more rope to tie her down.

She wriggled and screamed as to her fate. The man took the dagger from the table next to the throne and stretched his arm into a basket next to the slab and reached in and pulled out a cockerel. The satisfied pleasure shone in his face as he smoothly slit the throat of the bird. The unpleasant scene revealed itself to him, as the man let the warm blood drip, from the girls neck down to her feet.

His mouth was dry with fear but relieved

that the girl was unharmed, he managed to hide and conceal himself from this secret society.

After this strange act had been performed, the girl was freed and led away by one of the members, free he supposed until this bizarre show was acted out again. The cult dispersed lowering their hoods. Antonia turned and looked at Edmund with frightened eyes.

When this crazy spectacle had finished and he left the temple, when the coast was clear. He cautiously made his way back to his studio. Finally he could return to some sort of normality and ponder on what he had witnessed. He had really been fearful for the young girls life and relieved that it was a macabre theatrical performance.

He needed to get away from here but how? He needed to be paid for his work. He would once again speak to the sister of the Baron.

The diaries were still in the inside pocket of

his jacket and he was quite excited to see what was written inside them.

The first was dated 10th Sept when she was just thirteen.

That evening as he was sipping his glass of port, he heard a noise outside his door and then a gentle tap. It was Antonia.

'Edmund, I saw you today in the temple. The Baron knows you were there too, it's a dangerous game they are playing. They are dabbling in things you or I don't understand.' She went on, 'we need to get away, tonight. I got caught up with all this when I landed the part in Letters from Cane and now they won't let me leave the group, I have seen too much.'

'How were you caught up in it?'

'I wanted fame, I would do anything at the time. Everyone has a price Edmund and mine was this. They are performing a séance and are trying to conjure up spirits, I've seen it before in Brazil. You are the key don't you understand you restored the paintings, did you notice the thirteenth throne was empty?'

'Yes, there were twelve robed figures and thirteen stone chairs.'

'You are thirteen, don't you see? How do you think these people knew you had fallen on bad times? You are a member of The Club in Manchester?'

'Yes, it's a prestigious society, quite difficult to get in there.'

'The Baron is the Patron, some of the people you were mixing with are members of this group. Your price was set by the money lender. This was all a plan. You are naïve, you never checked, you just wanted your own gallery and you didn't care who lent you the money.'

'Do you know who lent me the money?'

'Edmund, you are the thirteenth. You are

about to be initiated as payment to cancel the debt.'

'Who financed the business Antonia? Tell me?'

Antonia went quiet.

'So there is no money? Is that what you are telling me? I have to go along with this?'

Edmund paced the floor, confounded and perturbed.

'The money lender, it's the man in the bowler hat, am I right?'

Antonia neither agreed nor disagreed, which confirmed Edmunds suspicion.

'It's a theatrical act, I witnessed it. I will go along with it, that way the debt will be cancelled and I will walk away a free man with no money chains.'

Antonia tried to change his mind and persuade him to leave immediately, she knew only too well that the dagger to be used on the unsuspecting victim, lured into a false sense of security by the drama the time before was going to be real and not that of a magicians tool.

She begged with him, 'Edmund you need to leave. It's not what it seems, these people… you don't know what they are capable of…'

He stopped her mid sentence she once again pierced his soul with her eyes. He couldn't help moving in for a kiss until.

A knock on the door startled the pair into a dignified straightening of behaviour. Edmund opened it to be gifted an envelope, an instruction to meet with the Baron that evening in the music room at 6pm.

Antonia, defeated as Edmund insisted he would attend retreated back to her suite, knowing that this would be a very serious move for Edmund. She would be present along with the twelve and part of this barbarous act.

Chapter Ten

Edmund lay on his bed, the window in his room letting a soft breeze gently sway the lace at his window. The outside scent pleasant to his nostrils. The sound of a magpie caw cawing into the late afternoon.

Excited and with a feeling of voyeurism he untied the string that held these secrets together. What was he to find? There was something sacred and precious about diaries and Edmund opened the first page. It was the Barons sister:

10th September

I have decided to start to write in my diary.

I was given this as a birthday present. I feel so old today. I'm now thirteen. No longer a child I think.

I have a crush on my brothers friend Richard. I don't know why, because he is so mean at times.

My brother threw a frog at his shoe and he kicked it with such force, that I ran away and cried so much for the poor innocent thing, how could anyone be so cruel.

Even though I cried, I still love him. I wish I didn't because I also hate him too.

20th May

We spent the afternoon in the summer house, I was going to ask Emily to make us up a picnic but he told me it was a secret so I bundled some cakes and some lemonade out from the kitchen into a basket and didn't tell anyone I was meeting Richard.

He can be so charming at times but he can

be hard work too.

I spoke to him for ages about anything and everything, he just listened and nodded. Why doesn't he speak more? He is so attractive. He is so dark and mysterious. I don't think my parents would like me meeting him in secret.

30th May

We went to the summer house again today, this time he asked me if I would mind if he kissed me. I didn't mind at all. He pressed me up roughly against the wall and put his lips on mine, I thought it would heaven but then he bit me. I'm never going to meet him secretly again.

And so the story carried on. An abusive relationship, she loving him and he playing her like a toy. The diaries unravelled that the man, the Barons friend was Richard the man in the Bowler hat.

Diary entries later spoke of her being enticed into an occultist game set up between Richard and her brother.

Deflowered aptly in the summer, her expectations dashed.

2nd July

He holds me so gently and guides me so softly, then so hatefully he hurts me. He drops and breaks me but I seem to be under his spell. He laughs when I plead with him, but I love his love. The scratches and bites and when I ask him to stop, he just carries on. He plays with my heart, body and mind. His words burn me like a hot poker. Ghastly pleasure. Why do I surrender to this, why can I not do without this torment. You are my cruel master, and then you call me your little kitten.

An abusive relationship unravelled. It made

for uncomfortable reading as she shared her innermost thoughts within the pages, Edmund carried on.

Her now more than wanting Richard, for not giving her enough. The love dance began. Backwards and forwards. He enticing her, then dropping her, she needy, as she danced forward, he danced backwards, this went on for years. She took some perverse pleasure in his cruelty with her. She had an expectation of being in love. Love was never to be pleasurable, it was always to be a thorn in her heart.

The society he was part of, held in esteem by the other members, she was never allowed to join. Although she had sufficient inheritance it was truly a gentlemen's club.

This gentleman's club were playing a dangerous game and as soon as she was caught up as a witness in the sacrificial acts, she was tied to this circle by blackmail.

It unravelled that her brother and Richard had a power over her and she was trapped here within these grand walls. A prisoner.

The sacrifice of fowls was grim but better than the sacrifice of that young girl, Edmund concluded, after witnessing that theatrical scene, the pact with them had certainly frightened the young girl terribly, but they had released her after all, he thought.

He was anxious to leave this place but he would go along with this stage show, as he was desperate to cut ties with these people, and the noose of the debt.

He hid the diaries under his pillow and made his way to meet The Baron.

Chapter Eleven

The Baron was stood in his smoking jacket with Richard. A sadistic glint in the eyes of the man in the bowler hat. The rules of the game were about to be explained to him as to what part he would play. It went something like this:

- He would be led into the room with the thirteen stone thrones.
- A young maiden would be brought in. It was explained that she had already played this game before as Edmund well knew.

- There, she would be tied with rope to a sacrificial stone and a fake dagger would be handed to him.
- He was to pierce the fake dagger through her heart, the blade, on sensing contact with skin would retract on impact. The girl would be safe.
- Warm cockerels blood would be poured onto her body and into a chalice.
- His head would be anointed and he was to drink from the cup.
- Initiation and baptism.
- He would take his throne and finally to the pairs delight he would be part of the golden order.

Today, he would never look back and would never want for anything again in his whole life. A small price to pay. He would be looked up to, with his promotion, and ascend his position in 'The Club' to Lodge master.

Prestige at last. These people were in a more than great position to help him and he had restored the artworks after all. Edmund was almost tempted to rub his hands together but on glancing at Richards face and cold presence behind them both he thought better of it. So, he just proceeded to listen with fascination.

He had decided to go along with this game. If he followed all the instructions, then, he would be guided,he had a full guarantee that all his debts were to be paid off in full.

Richard, all the while, sat behind them both. He had never been so disturbed by another human being in his life. His mind wandered from the moment, and thought back to the diaries that were fresh in his mind. From the entries, he knew of this mans capabilities. He took evil to the extreme but just to the brink, and had a clever way of being able to redeem himself in some kind of perverse way.

So that was the day, that Edmund agreed to the dance with the devil.

Prestige, status, recognition and no debt.

His robes were laid out for him and this bizarre game began. Part of him felt an excitement to be initiated into of this group, groomed and fascinated, he did as he was told.

Immediately on adorning the cloak he had agreed to play a role in this macabre stage show.

Chapter Twelve

The room had been dressed in soft white drapes, a lamp lit by oil was throwing shadows all over the place.

Intrigued he glanced at the others, heads down cloaked.

Rain hammered three narrow windows set high into the stone walls. The lightening zigzagged like a firecracker across the night sky, lighting up the dust within the shadows.

Clouds boiled outside as Edmund braced himself for what was to come. Equal amounts of fear and excitement took hold of him and he found he had to take a couple of deep breaths to calm himself, as his very thoughts set him on edge. Fear of the unknown, the excitement to be involved. He shifted uncomfortably as he wished he had relieved his bladder before entering.

Hypnotic chanting commenced, a ceremony. Mesmerising, time slipped by, like oil from a broken jar.

Edmunds eyes were drawn to the back of the stone slab, just in front of the ornate box. A large candelabra, carved with entwined twisted bodies as they devoured each other.

Silence fell as the stifled sobs and cries of a girl, as she was dragged into the room. One of the dogs howled in the distance as the maiden was roughly disrobed and made to kneel in front of the master.

The master lifted the dagger, licked the steel and drew blood, he caressed the large blade with his fingers and gleamed with pleasure as his sleeve seeped a scarlet hue.

Edmund was ordered to step forward and take his place between the two. A dagger, the very same he had seen in the art work, the eye of the Egyptian, jewelled and ornate, surprised, as the weight was quite heavy, it would take little effort to enter the skin of the young victim, the blade would retract upon touch he had been assured. A chant began.

Tas eeris eeris kaa, eeris kaa,

Aka aka,

Tas eeris, eeris kaa, eeris kaa,

Aka aka

Repeated over and over again.

Edmund found the sound enchanting and it was easy to repeat so he joined in.

Bodies swayed to the rhythm as they created this hypnotic music.

The girls eyes shone with fear and she pleaded with him to stop, he knew she was part of this game, this very enticing game. She was good! A good actress he thought.

This game disturbed and excited him in a strange way.

She was convincing though, he was enchanted by the mood of this group, he smiled at her and lifted the blade high into the air. He would be admired for his performance and he let himself be drawn forward. A sacrifice and he was playing the lead actor in this fabulous stage production.

A small doubt invaded his thought, what if the mechanism was faulty, what then? He quickly pushed that thought away as he was there and in the moment.

A look from the master, as he nodded for the blade to strike the child and Edmund was more than ready. Glinting on the blade, the candles lit up like silver slivers as the metal came slashing down, A scream pierced the air, it jolted Edmund from his trance.

Drapes ablaze. Paraffin oil trickled towards the altar as the sound of the oil lamp crashed.

Chaos! Everyone ran for safety. Antonia tugged, pleaded and dragged Edmund towards an opening at the side of the chapel. The heat seared his skin as he ran back to untie the girl, fighting off flames, more than three times he returned, before fleeing with the girl in tow.

Running towards the opening, the flames engulfed the whole space.

As this place went up in flames all hands were on deck, from the butler to the groundsmen, frantic to put out and quench these flames. Worried for their livelihoods. If this place burnt to cinders, they would be without jobs.

Luck was on his side as the vehicles had been left unattended, the owner, in a false sense security, had left their keys within these vehicles, they managed to flee, he, Antonia and the girl.

The authorities would never be informed as there was too much at stake.

Antonia's career as an actress.

The shame the maiden thought she may bring on her Family. The fact she might not gain employment elsewhere if she exposed them.

Edmunds status as an art dealer and restorer.

Not one of them were willing to speak; all silenced by their own conscience and for whatever reason, from their own free will, choosing to go along and take part in this lurid game of gloom.

Chapter Thirteen

As Edmund turned the key to his gallery in Lever Street. Happy to be free from his debt; Happy to have paid his dues to the Baron. Even happier to have escaped.

On entering his premises, he was shocked as the first thing he saw, was no other than *The Sacrifice* by Albert Barolo Francis a thirteenth piece that Edmund had no idea existed, a priceless painting that made him shiver down to his bones. This was a final part of the collection of the sacrifice of a young girl.

The blade entered just below the rib cage. Blood seeping from this wound, eyes wide open, disturbing, the eyes wide; as she met her destiny. A hooded robed figure penetrating this young female with a blade. Thirteen robed figures in all.

The man with the blade wore the same robes as Edmund.

Antonia had changed fate by accidentally setting the place ablaze. By falling onto the paraffin lamp.

This wasn't as it should be and suddenly he became afraid that this wasn't the last he was going to hear from this pact.

He hadn't wanted this at all. He had hoped this would be the end of his contract with them. He was feeling anxious as his inner voice screamed to him to be very careful. These were dangerous people and this wasn't over yet.

He needed to think about things, he needed a drink. 'The Club' was the last place he wanted to go to as he knew of its connections with the Baron. He had read in the gazette that Victor had been engulfed in the accident. Eleanor had been burnt, but survived.

He made his way to a pub just further on from the 'The Club' an establishment called The Manchester Tavern. The night was brisk and he pulled his gaberdine coat collar around his neck to stave off the piercing wind. On he went, as the glass of beer beckoned him on.

As he walked past 'The Club' he made out the distinct Silhouette of the man in the Bowler hat. Richard, was making his way up the steps. Edmund stopped in his tracks.

The bowler hat, turned and looked directly at Edmund, Edmund put his head down and continued on briskly to the warmth and comfort of the Manchester tavern.

Seated with his long awaited pint, he breathed deeply and contemplated his thoughts. Antonia, she had helped him.

The girl he had freed her, but his soul wasn't free.

He realised there are Facets to everyone's personality. If he would have done as he was asked he would have murdered the girl. Had he been that naïve to believe the blade would retract. No, what disturbed him mostly was the feeling of power and control his role had given him.

Murder on the other hand disgusted him, but the initiation into this pact brought out a dark side in him, a powerful feeling, with an ego massaged, he was troubled and disturbed more than ever.

As he argued with himself and contemplated these dark feelings, the door of the Manchester Tavern opened and in walked Richard.

Edmund felt a heavy weight upon his chest, there was never going to be friendship between the two, and having read the diaries, and the unscrupulous ways he had manipulated Eleanor, now disfigured, was unimaginable.

This man did not have a friendly bone within his whole body. Just as anticipated the man made his way to Edmunds table and without an invitation, pulled out a chair and abruptly joined him.

The conversation started icily. A bowler hat placed between the two, Richard spoke.

So, this is how the story goes.

Edmund was to be part of this group whether he liked it or not. The debt was paid as long as the gallery was used for regular meetings.

There would be lords, of lodges, meetings once a month, and he would be expected to host. The painting would be his and the debt sorted out, as long as

Edmund did as he was told, and kept his

mouth shut. Richard drew his finger to his lip, he sealed the deal as he gestured, smiled and shushed him, he reassured Edmund the initiation would proceed as planned.

An art dealer, despondent, defeated, and backed into a corner, with no other choice but to surrender to the powerful.

Richard, escorted Edmund away from the pub, his hand gripped his shoulder in a clasp, he was led and welcomed back with with open arms and much admiration from the prestigious members of 'The Club'. He was seated in the lodge's main chair. A golden chain adorned around his neck. A sceptre placed in his right hand and an Egyptian eye in his left.

'What led a fool to dance with the Devil?'

Printed in Poland
by Amazon Fulfillment
Poland Sp. z o.o., Wrocław